I KNOW A WEE PIGGY

by Kim Norman   pictures by Henry Cole

SCHOLASTIC INC.

For my dear Doris and Atwill,
and our beautiful Smithfield –K.N.

For Massimo Cesare Chirighin
...augurandovi molte avventure felici! –H.C.

ISBN 978-0-545-85270-8

12 11 10 9 8 7 6 5 4 3 2 1   15 16 17 18 19 20/0

Printed in the U.S.A.   40

First Scholastic printing, January 2015

Text set in Coop Light
The artwork was created in acrylic paints and colored pencil on Arches hot press watercolor paper.

I know a wee piggy . . .

who wallowed in **BROWN**.

Upside down, he wallowed in **brown**.

"But **brown** is not for me," he said. "I think I'll add a rinse of . . ."

RED!

I know a wee piggy who wallowed in **red**.
Hoof to head, he wallowed in **red**.

He wallowed in **red** to go with the **brown**.
Upside down, he wallowed in **brown**.

Piggy said, "The **red's** too bright. I think I'll add a wash of . . ."

WHITE!

I know a wee piggy who wallowed in white.
It's not polite to wallow in white.

He wallowed in white to go with the **red**.
He wallowed in **red** to go with the **brown**.
Upside down, he wallowed in **brown**.

Piggy said, "Too pale, I think. I'd better add a pinch of . . ."

PINK!

I know a wee piggy who wallowed in pink.
How silly to think he needed more pink.

He wallowed in pink to go with the white.
He wallowed in white to go with the red.
He wallowed in red to go with the brown.
Upside down, he wallowed in brown.

"Pink's a bore!" I heard him bellow. "I need about a yard of . . ."

YELLOW!

I know a wee piggy who wallowed in yellow.
Slippery fellow, to wallow in yellow.

He wallowed in yellow to go with the pink.
He wallowed in pink to go with the white.
He wallowed in white to go with the red.
He wallowed in red to go with the brown.
Upside down, he wallowed in brown.

Piggy squealed, "I won't look back until I add a blast of . . ."

BLACK!

I know a wee piggy who wallowed in **black**.
Out by a shack, he wallowed in **black**.

He wallowed in **black** to go with the yellow.
He wallowed in yellow to go with the pink.
He wallowed in pink to go with the white.
He wallowed in white to go with the red.
He wallowed in red to go with the brown.
Upside down, he wallowed in **brown**.

Piggy shouted, "Now I've seen that I should add a glimpse of . . ."

GREEN!

I know a wee piggy who wallowed in **green**.
Oh, what a scene! He'll NEVER get clean!

He wallowed in **green** to go with the **black**.
He wallowed in **black** to go with the yellow.
He wallowed in yellow to go with the **pink**.
He wallowed in **pink** to go with the white.
He wallowed in white to go with the **red**.
He wallowed in **red** to go with the **brown**.
Upside down, he wallowed in **brown**.

Piggy sighed. "The **green's** okay, but now I need a glob of . . ."

GRAY!

I know a wee piggy who wallowed in **gray**.
Orange and **gray**, a brilliant display.

UH-OH . . .

GET OUT
OF HIS WAY!

I know a wee piggy who didn't stop there. . . .

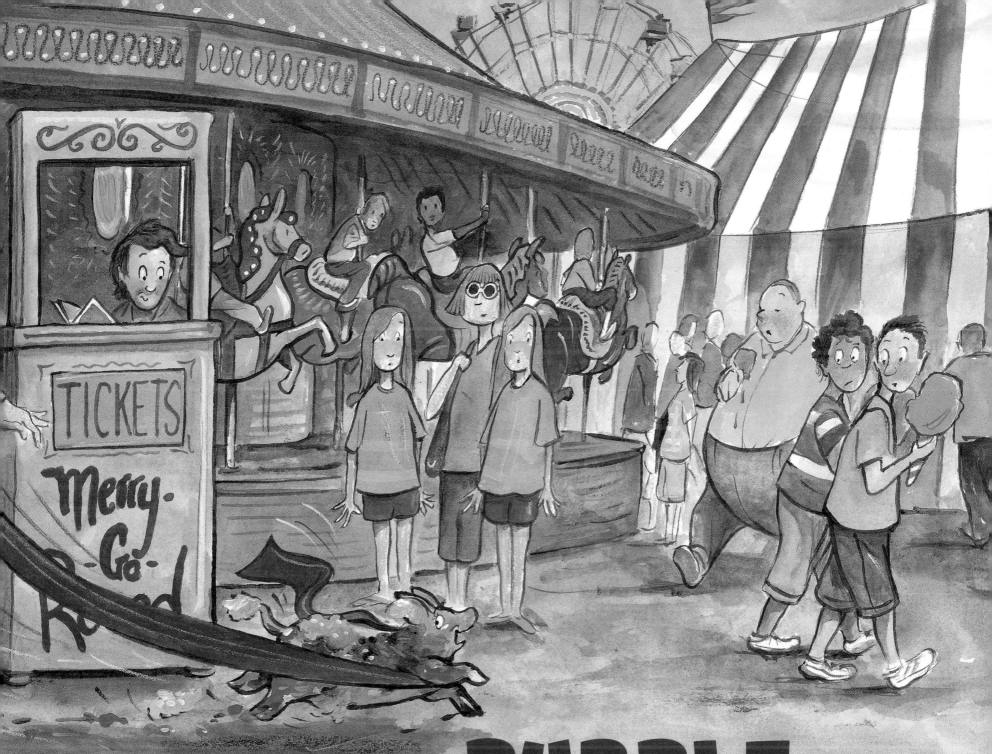

He wallowed in **PURPLE** . . .

ALL OVER THE FAIR!

He added the **purple** . . .

. . . to go with the **gray**.

He added the **gray** . . .

. . . to go with the **green**.

He added the **green** . . .

. . . to go with the **black**.

He added the **black** . . .

. . . to go with the yellow.

He added the yellow . . .

. . . to go with the pink.

He added the pink . . .

. . . to go with the white.

He added the white . . .

. . . to go with the red.

He added the red . . .

. . . to go with the brown.

Upside down, he wallowed in brown.

Piggy said, "I'm not quite through. I won't be till I add some . . ."

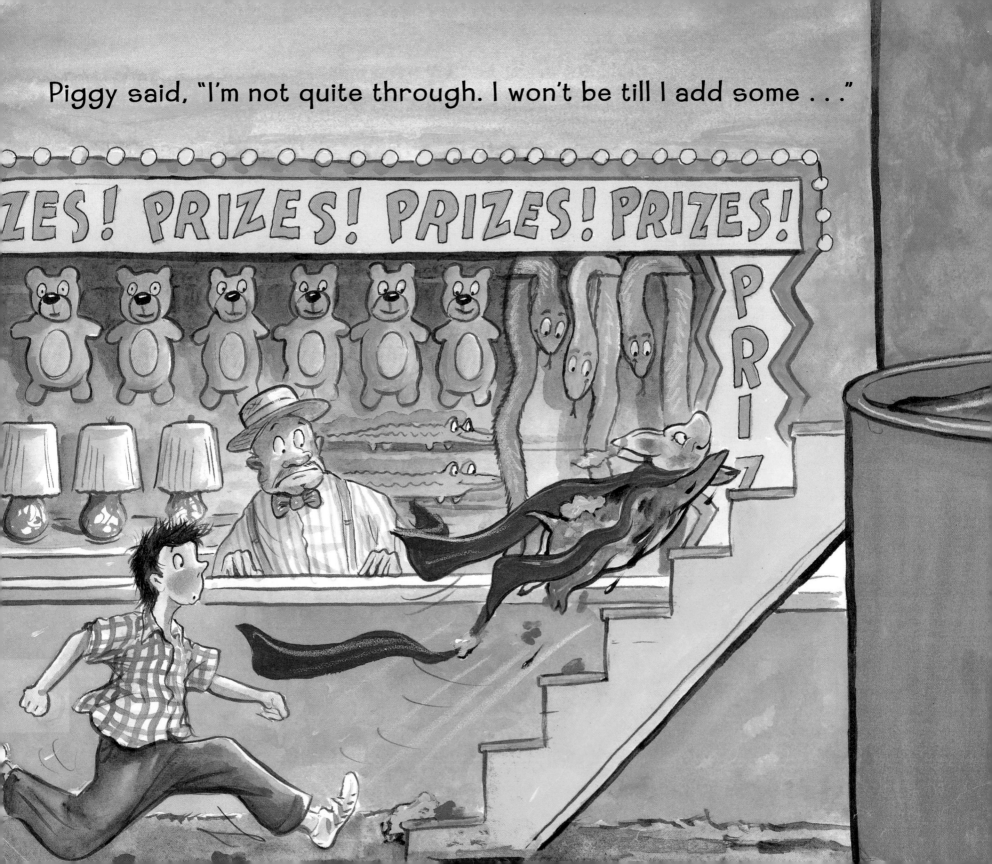

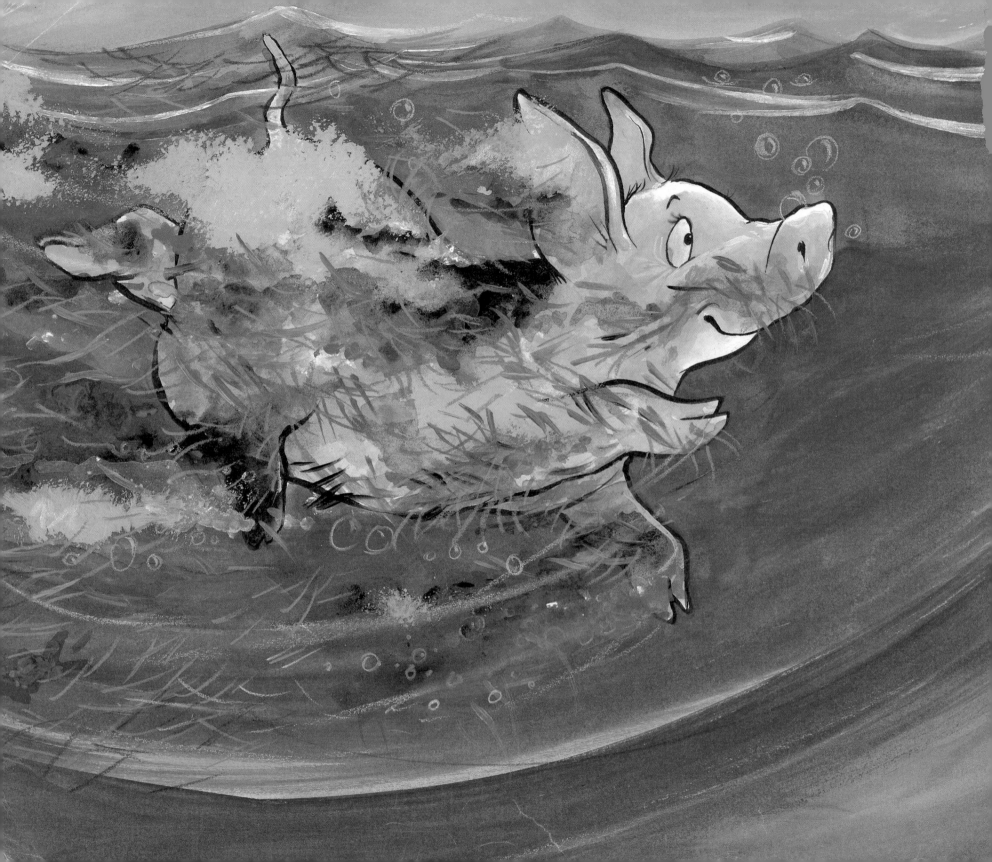

BLUE!

I know a wee piggy who wallowed in **blue**. . . .

He won it, too!